Join the Little Golden Books®
Billion Golden Memories Celebration

2 GRAND PRIZES:
7-day Cruise to the Caribbean for a family of 4 (two adults and two children) including round-trip airfare and stateroom accommodations plus $2,000 cash

$100,000 in prizes!

6 FIRST PRIZES:
Zenith® Home Video Entertainment Center (TV, VCR, Video Camcorder)

12 SECOND PRIZES:
Zenith® Video Cassette Recorder **plus** 12 Golden Book Video® Cassettes

40 THIRD PRIZES:
Zenith® 9" DeLights Color TV

500 FOURTH PRIZES:
Set of 8 Golden Junior Classic™ Storybooks

——————— PLUS ———————

7,000 BONUS PRIZES*:
$4.95 Golden® Storybook

* Bonus prize for the first 7,000 consumers to share their favorite memory of Little Golden Books with us.

TO ENTER:
Just complete the official entry form** found in each specially marked Little Golden Book, First Little Golden Book® and Big Little Golden Book® displaying the "BILLION GOLDEN® MEMORIES" symbol on its cover.

** NO PURCHASE NECESSARY TO ENTER. See sweepstakes rule #2 for alternate entry requirements.

BONUS!
**Favorite Golden®
Memories Offer**
turn page for details

Official Entry Form	Submit by December 31, 1987

Join the Little Golden Books®
Billion Golden Memories Celebration

Send this completed form to:

BILLION GOLDEN MEMORIES CELEBRATION
Dept. 9045 • Wheeling, IL 60090

Please tell us the title of your favorite Little Golden Book®:

_____
(PLEASE PRINT OR TYPE)

Name: _____

Address: _____

City: _____ State: _____ Zip: _____

Only One Entry Per Envelope. Enter as often as you wish, but use only official entry forms or alternate entry forms. Mechanically reproduced entries and photocopies are not permitted. *Each* entry must be sent separately via First Class mail in a #10 letter size envelope and be received *no later than December 31, 1987.* Offer good only in U.S.A.

a Billion Golden Memories

──Favorite Golden®Memories BONUS Offer!──

Share your favorite memory of Little Golden Books® with us and you'll get *a FREE book worth at least $4.95* (offer is limited to the first 7,000 responses). Just hand-print or type your name, address, city, state, zip code and telephone number (including area code) along with your fondest memory of Little Golden Books on a page of 8½" x 11" paper. Memories must be a minimum of 25 words. Then, send the sheet with your memory to: **MY FAVORITE MEMORY OF LITTLE GOLDEN BOOKS P.O. Box 1410, Wheeling, IL 60090**

PLEASE NOTE: *All* memories *must* be typed or hand-printed and become the property of Western Publishing Company, Inc. Limit one bonus prize per name, address or household. By submitting your fondest memory of Little Golden Books, you consent to the use of your submission, name and likeness for advertising, promotion, public relations or trade purposes with no additional compensation. *DO NOT INCLUDE YOUR FONDEST MEMORY OF LITTLE GOLDEN BOOKS WITH YOUR SWEEPSTAKES ENTRY FORM.*

Billion Golden®Memories Celebration

OFFICIAL RULES

NO PURCHASE NECESSARY TO ENTER

1. **TO ENTER,** simply write the title of your favorite LITTLE GOLDEN BOOK® on the entry certificate from the inside first page of each selected Little Golden Book, First Little Golden Book® or Big Little Golden Book® displaying the special "BILLION GOLDEN® MEMORIES" symbol on its cover. Then, complete your official entry form (hand-print or type) and mail it to:
   BILLION GOLDEN MEMORIES CELEBRATION Dept. 9045, Wheeling, IL 60090

2. **TO RECEIVE AN ALTERNATE ENTRY FORM WITHOUT MAKING A PURCHASE,** simply send a self-addressed #10 letter size stamped envelope by November 1, 1987 to:
   BILLION GOLDEN MEMORIES CELEBRATION ALTERNATE ENTRY FORM P.O. Box 1410, Wheeling, IL 60090

   Alternate entry forms are only available while *supplies last.* One official alternate entry form will be sent per envelope. Residents of the states of Washington and Vermont need not include postage.

3. Enter as often as you wish, but use only official entry forms or alternate entry forms. Mechanically reproduced entries and photocopies are not permitted. *Each* entry must be sent separately via First Class mail in a #10 letter size envelope and must be received *no later than December 31, 1987.* Mail each entry to:
   BILLION GOLDEN MEMORIES CELEBRATION Dept. 9045, Wheeling, IL 60090

4. Prizes to be awarded include **2 GRAND PRIZES:** 7-day Cruise to the Caribbean for a family of 4 (two adults and two children) including round trip airfare via coach or special fare, double occupancy stateroom accommodations (Trip *must* be taken before November 15,1988) plus $2,000 cash, worth approximately $6,000* each; **6 FIRST PRIZES:** Zenith® Home Video Entertainment Center (25" Stereo Color TV, VCR, Video Camcorder) valued at $2,504* each; **12 SECOND PRIZES:** Zenith® Video Cassette Recorder plus 12 Golden Book Video™ Cassettes worth $629* each; **40 THIRD PRIZES:** Zenith® 9" DeLights Television worth $259* each; **500 FOURTH PRIZES:** Set of 8 Golden Junior Classic™ storybooks valued at $40* per set. **7,000 BONUS PRIZES:** Golden® Story Book worth $4.95* each. Total prizes are valued at approximately $100,000*. Merchandise prize deliveries are limited to the U.S.
   *Market value as of November, 1986.

5. *The first 7,000 consumers to hand-print or type their name, address, city, state, zip code and telephone number (including area code) along with their fondest memory of Little Golden Books on a sheet of 8½" x 11" paper will receive a FREE book from Western Publishing Company, Inc. worth at least $4.95. Memories must be a minimum of 25 words.*

Each memory must be sent in a separate envelope to:
   MY FAVORITE MEMORY OF LITTLE GOLDEN BOOKS
   P.O. Box 1410, Wheeling, IL 60090
Only one bonus prize per name, address or household. All entries become the property of Western Publishing Company, Inc. By submitting your fondest memory of Little Golden Books, you consent to the use of your submission, name and likeness for advertising, promotion, public relations or trade purposes with no additional compensation. Do not include your official or alternate sweepstakes entry form with this submission.

6. Sweepstakes begins March 1, 1987 or whenever first entry is received and ends December 31, 1987. Sponsor is not responsible for late, lost, misdirected, mutilated or stolen entries via mail. Entries will be randomly selected by David Kessler & Associates, Inc., an independent judging agency whose decisions are final on all matters relating to this sweepstakes. Drawing to be held during the week of January 25, 1988. All prizes will be awarded. Odds of winning based on number of entries received. Only one prize per household. Prizes are non-transferable and no substitutions are allowed. Travel arrangements and accommodations are by sponsor's choice. Taxes on each prize are the sole responsibility of the respective winners. Winners will be notified by March 1, 1988. The winners will be notified by mail and may be required to sign and return an affidavit of eligibility and release from liability within thirty (30) days of notification. Alternate winners will be selected in the event of non-compliance or the return of any undeliverable prize or notification of prize award.

7. Sweepstakes open to all residents of the U.S. Employees and their immediate family members of Western Publishing Company, Inc., its affiliates, participating retailers, agencies, contractors associated with this sweepstakes and David Kessler and Associates, Inc., are not eligible. All prizes will be awarded to a parent or legal guardian if the winner is a minor. By entering, winners consent to the use of their names and likenesses for advertising, promotion, public relations or trade purposes with no additional compensation. If a prize is not generally available at the end of the contest, a substitution of equal or greater value will be made. Void where prohibited by law and subject to all Federal, state and local regulations.

8. For a list of major winners, send a self-addressed #10 letter size stamped envelope to:
   BILLION GOLDEN MEMORIES CELEBRATION WINNERS LIST P.O. Box 1410, Wheeling, IL 60090
Do not include request for the winner's list with your sweepstakes entry.

Sponsor: Western Publishing Company, Inc. Racine, Wisconsin 53404

FIRST CLASS

INSURED

VIA AIR MAIL

VIA AIR MAIL

AIR MAIL 6¢

U.S. POSTAGE

Seven Little Postmen

BY MARGARET WISE BROWN
AND EDITH THACHER HURD

CONTENTS — MERCHANDISE
POSTMASTER — THIS PARCEL
MAY BE OPENED FOR POSTAL
INSPECTION IF NECESSARY
RETURN POSTAGE GUARANTEED

FRAGILE

Pictures by
TIBOR GERGELY

A GOLDEN BOOK • New York
Western Publishing Company, Inc.
Racine, Wisconsin 53404

SPECIAL DELIVERY

A boy had a secret. It was a surprise.
He wanted to tell his grandmother.
So he sent his secret through the mail.
The story of that letter
Is the reason for this tale
Of the seven little postmen who carried the mail.

Because there was a secret in the letter
The boy sealed it with red sealing wax.
If anyone broke the seal
The secret would be out.

He slipped the letter into the mail box.

The first little postman
Took it from the box,
Put it in his bag,
And walked seventeen blocks
To a big Post Office
All built of rocks.

The letter with the secret
Was dumped on a table
With big and small letters
That all needed the label
Of the big Post Office.

Stamp stamp, clickety click,
The machinery ran with a quick sharp tick.
The letter with the secret is stamped at last
And the round black circle tells that it passed
Through the cancelling machine
    Click   whizz   fast!

Big letters
Small letters
Thin and tall—
The second little postman
Sorts them all.
The letters are sorted
From East to West
From North to South.

"And this letter
Had best go West,"
Said the second
Little postman,
Scratching his chest.
Into the pouch
Lock it tight
The secret letter
Must travel all night.

The third little postman in the big mail car
Comes to a crossroad where waiting are
A green, a yellow, and a purple car.
They all stop there. There is nothing to say.
The mail truck has the right of way!
"The mail must go through!"

Up and away through sleet and hail
This airplane carries the fastest mail.
The pilot flies through whirling snow
As far and as fast as the plane can go.

The mail is landed for the evening train.
Now hang the pouch on the big hook crane!
The engine speeds up the shining rails
And the fourth little postman
Grabs the mail with a giant hook.

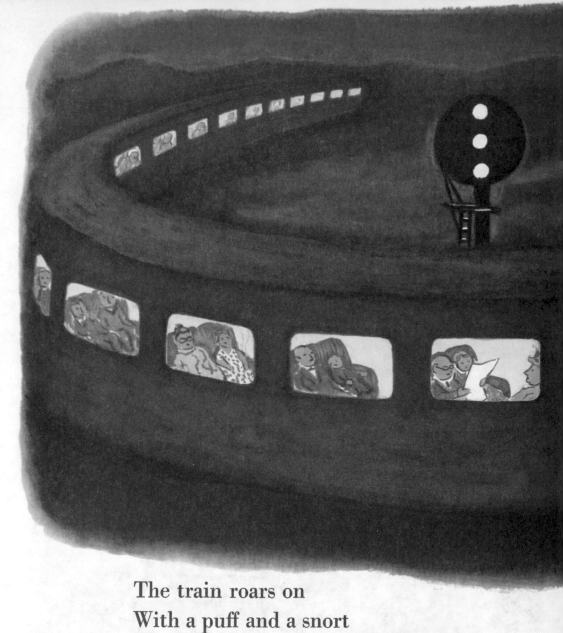

The train roars on
With a puff and a snort
And the fourth little postman
Begins to sort.

The train carries the letter
Through gloom of night
In a mail car filled with electric light

To a country postman
By a country road
Where the fifth little postman
Is waiting for his load.

The mail clerk
Heaves the mail pouch
With all his might
To the fifth little postman
Who grabs it tight.

Then off he goes
Along the lane
And over the hill
Until
He comes to a little town
That is very small—
So very small
The Post Office there
Is hardly one at all.

The sixth little postman
In great big boots
Sorts the letters
For their various routes—
Some down the river,
Some over the hill.

But the secret letter
Goes farther still.

The seventh little postman on R.F.D.
Carries letters and papers, chickens and fruit
To the people who live along his route.

He stops to deliver some sugar
To Mr. Jones who keeps a store
And always seems to need something more.

For Mrs. O'Finnigan with all her ills
He brings a bottle of bright pink pills.

There was a funny post card
For a little boy
Playing in his own backyard.

There was something for Sally
And something for Sam

And something for Mrs. Potter
Who was busy making jam.

There were dozens of chickens
For Mrs. Pickens

And a dress for a party
For Mrs. McCarty.

At the last house along the way sat the grandmother of the boy who had sent the letter with the secret in it. She had been wishing all day he would come to visit. For she lived all alone in a tiny house and sometimes felt quite lonely.

The Postman blew his whistle and gave her the letter with the red sealing wax on it — the secret letter!

"Sakes alive! What is it about?"
Sakes alive! The secret is out!
What does it say?

SEVEN LITTLE POSTMEN

Seven Little Postmen carried the mail
Through Rain and Snow and Wind and Hail
Through Snow and Rain and Gloom of Night

Seven Little Postmen
Out of sight.
Over Land and Sea
Through Air and Light
Through Snow and Rain
And Gloom of Night—
Put a stamp on your letter
And seal it tight.

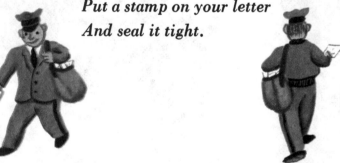